SESAME STREET

I Want to Be
A
DOCTOR

By Liza Alexander
Illustrated by Lauren Attinello

A SESAME STREET/GOLDEN PRESS BOOK
Published by Western Publishing Company, Inc.,
in conjunction with Children's Television Workshop.

One day I went to visit Granny Bird. She gave me a
big hug and a kiss on the beak. But something awful
happened when Granny went up the stairs with my
suitcase. Just as she got to the top, she tripped and fell—
THUNK!

"Granny! Are you all right?" I asked.

"Yes, dear," she said, "but I've hurt my ankle. Be a
good bird and run next door and see if Dr. Fuzzle is
home."

"Don't worry, Granny!" I said. "I'll be right back!"

KNOCK, KNOCK! I pounded on the Fuzzles' door.
One of the little Fuzzles and his mommy opened it.

"Is the doctor in?" I asked.

"Yes," said the mommy, "I'm the doctor. You must be
Mrs. Bird's grandson."

"That's right," I said. "How did you know?"

Then I told her all about Granny's fall, and she
asked me to wait a minute while she got her bag.

As we walked back to Granny's I asked Dr. Fuzzle, "What's inside your black bag?"

"My medical instruments," she answered.

So I said, "You mean like a violin and a piano?"

Dr. Fuzzle laughed and said, "No, different kinds of instruments—tools that doctors use. You'll see what's inside the bag when I examine your granny."

"Examine? What does that mean?" I asked.

"Examine means to look closely," the doctor told me. "When I examine your granny's ankle, I will feel it and try to understand what's wrong."

Granny was sitting in the same spot at the top of the stairs.

"Now, let's see, Mrs. Bird," said Dr. Fuzzle. "Yes. Your ankle is swollen. Does it hurt a lot or just a little?"

"It hurts a lot," said Granny.

Dr. Fuzzle moved Granny's foot gently from side to side. Then she said, "Tell me if this is painful."

"Ouch," said Granny. "That hurts."

Next Dr. Fuzzle asked me to help Granny to bed.
Granny leaned on us like we were crutches and hopped
on her one good leg to her room.

I smoothed Granny's blanket and plumped her pillows. "Thank you, dear," she said, and I felt good because I was taking care of Granny!

The doctor told us she thought that Granny's ankle was probably sprained, not broken. Then Dr. Fuzzle let me help wrap Granny's ankle in a bandage.

When we finished the bandaging, the doctor told
Granny to put ice on her ankle and to keep her leg up.
Dr. Fuzzle also told us to come to her office the next
day so Granny's ankle could be X-rayed. Then
Dr. Fuzzle said good night and went home.

Granny stayed in bed, so I brought our dinner up to her room on a tray.

Then I washed the dishes all by myself!

I went upstairs and made sure Granny was okay. Then I tucked her in and gave her a kiss good night and went to bed myself. Boy, oh, boy, was I tired!

The next morning I was quite the early bird! I brought Granny breakfast in bed. She said it was delicious. I felt proud!

Then Granny asked me to find a cane in the back of her closet. Next I helped her get dressed.

We were ready to go. Granny told me to call a taxi, and we were off to Dr. Fuzzle's office.

Dr. Fuzzle took us straight to the X-ray room. She told us, "The X-ray machine is actually a big camera. We'll use it to take a picture of the bones inside your leg, Mrs. Bird."

Then the doctor lowered the big X-ray machine and switched it on and off—CLICK.

Then I asked the doctor, "Are you going to *examine* Granny now?"

"That's right, Big Bird," she said. "While we wait for the X-rays to develop, I'll give you a quick checkup, Mrs. Bird. All right?"

"Fine and dandy," said Granny.

The doctor was wearing a funny-looking necktie.
She plugged it into her ears and held the bottom against
Granny's chest. "What's that?" I asked.

"It's a stethoscope," said Dr. Fuzzle.

So I said it, too, "STETH-O-SCOPE." Then the
doctor gave it to me so I could listen to Granny's heart,
also. Her heart went *kathump-kathump-kathump,* and it
was loud!

Then the doctor held an ice-cream-stick thing called
a tongue depressor on Granny's tongue. She looked
down Granny's throat with a tiny flashlight.

"Very fine!" said the doctor.

"And this is an otoscope," said Dr. Fuzzle. "It helps me see that the passages inside your ear are clear, Mrs. Bird."

"Glad to *hear* it," said Granny, and we all laughed.

After that the doctor wrapped a cuff around Granny's wing and squeezed a little bulb. The cuff filled up with air like a water wing. "I am measuring your blood pressure."

"How is it?" asked Granny.

"Your blood pressure is just right," answered the doctor.

"Way to go, Granny!" I said.

Then a nurse came in and showed us the X-ray of Granny's ankle bones!

"Just as I thought," said Dr. Fuzzle. "No broken bones. Still, Mrs. Bird, stay off your feet as much as possible in the next few days so the sprain can heal. I'll give you some crutches so your ankle won't hurt so much."

"Dr. Fuzzle," I said, "I want to take X-ray pictures and carry a black bag with instruments in it. I want to listen to hearts with a stethoscope and examine people and birds and monsters. I want to be just like you!"

"Actually, Big Bird, you're already a lot like me," said Dr. Fuzzle. "Doctors help sick people and are curious about how bodies work."

Then Dr. Fuzzle showed me her medical school
diploma. That's where she learned how to be a doctor.
The diploma was framed on the wall and had a gold
seal like a first prize!

Soon it was time to go. Granny and I said, "So long!"

When we got home, Granny said, "I have an early birthday present for you, dear."

It was a black doctor's bag like Dr. Fuzzle's. Inside were toy medical instruments!

"Thank you for taking such good care of me," said Granny.

"I like taking care of you, Granny," I said. "And I need the practice. Because when I grow up, I want to be a doctor!"